BRADFORD PUBLIC LIBRARY
222-4536

ABBREVIATED REGULATIONS

1. Books may be kept two weeks.

2. For each book kept over time a fine of ~~two~~ cents a day will be imposed.

3. Pen or pencil marks, or leaf corners turned down, will be subject to a fine.

4. Persons taking books will be held responsible for their loss or injury.

5. No book is to be loaned to persons outside of the household.

6. Quiet and orderly deportment in the Library building is enjoined.

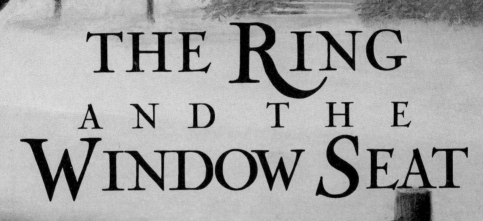

THE RING
AND THE
WINDOW SEAT

by Amy Hest

illustrated by Deborah Haeffele

SCHOLASTIC
HARDCOVER

SCHOLASTIC INC.
NEW YORK

Library of Congress Cataloging-in-Publication Data

Hest, Amy
  The ring and the window seat.

  Summary: Although she has been saving for a ring, Stella decides to give her bundle of nickels to a
carpenter who is trying to rescue his little girl from a war-torn country.
  [1. Generosity—Fiction] I. Haeffele, Deborah, ill. II. Title.
PZ7.H4375Ri   1990   [E]   88-4634

ISBN 0-590-41350-3

12 11 10 9 8 7 6 5 4 3 2 1   0 1 2 3 4 5/9
                                                    36

Printed in the U.S.A.

First Scholastic printing, November 1990

For Dianne —A.H.

To Steven, Christiane, and Cathryn
with love —D.H.

Aunt Stella's about as old as you can get. Her hair is winter-white and feathered lines around her eyes crinkle like tissue paper on Christmas morning. We live down the hill and up another hill from her house. She tells the best stories and she's my favorite person in all the world.

It is finally my birthday. Early morning sun-lines slip through branches of full summer trees and I am running to Aunt Stella. "Hello up there!" I call to her window.

I find her reading, always reading, on the cushioned window seat with five big pillows all around. "Happy birthday, Annie." She slides her magnifying glass between the pages of today's fat book, so I don't notice about her eyes getting worse.

"Will you come to my party?" I say.

"Haven't missed one yet. I'll be there at four."

I squeeze beside her and kiss her cheek. "Tell me a story. Please, Aunt Stella. A real one about *you* when you were a girl."

"How about the snake-in-the-kitchen story?"

"No way! Not on my birthday!"

"There's the one about the kitten I found in the woods...."

"You told it last time," I remind her.

"In that case, I've got just the one." She rearranges her legs and I breathe in her faint lemon scent, curling my warm toes against her cold bent ones. And she begins:

Long ago, when I was a girl in this house, I used to have birthday parties at the end of every summer. Grand parties, Annie, with hats and treasure hunts and a few best friends to share a cake with icing. One year was different, though. It was the year of the ring. And, the year of the window seat.

Oh that ring! It appeared one day, just like that, in the window of Winston's, my favorite shop in town. Don't you know, it was the most beautiful ring I'd ever seen—thinnest gold with a centered heart of darker gold—and I wanted it more than anything. But times were bad, and my parents had no money for rings.

So I started saving. Nickel by nickel. In a bright green sock tied up top with a tiny red bow, like a pouch. I saved and counted, for weeks and months, and the day before my birthday, at last, there were just enough. I would race to Winston's in the early morning, and wear the ring to my party!

But Annie! When I woke up, the sky was black and gray instead of blue and pink. Then came the rain—and what a rain it was—with hurricane winds that pushed the trees first one way and then the other. Then back again the first way.

"A storm is no place for a little girl," said my parents. "The ring must wait for another day."

"That's not fair!" I was mad.

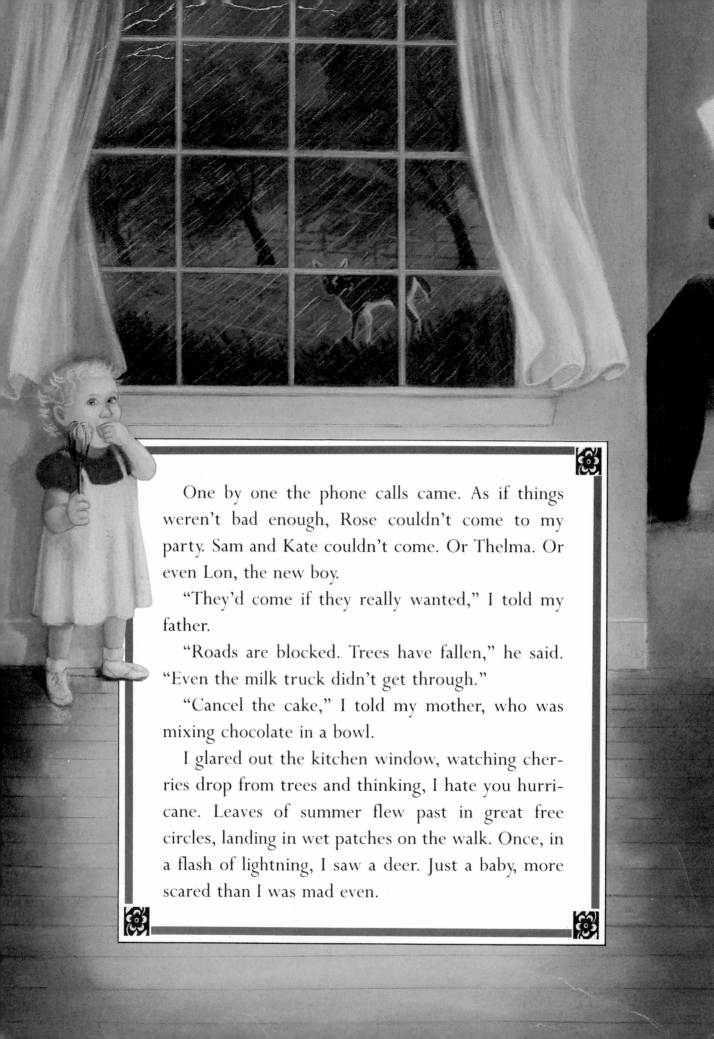

One by one the phone calls came. As if things weren't bad enough, Rose couldn't come to my party. Sam and Kate couldn't come. Or Thelma. Or even Lon, the new boy.

"They'd come if they really wanted," I told my father.

"Roads are blocked. Trees have fallen," he said. "Even the milk truck didn't get through."

"Cancel the cake," I told my mother, who was mixing chocolate in a bowl.

I glared out the kitchen window, watching cherries drop from trees and thinking, I hate you hurricane. Leaves of summer flew past in great free circles, landing in wet patches on the walk. Once, in a flash of lightning, I saw a deer. Just a baby, more scared than I was mad even.

Soon after there was a knock on the porch door. A man with eyes like sad blue satin stood there dripping pools of water on the polished wood floor. He was a carpenter, he said; George Rog was his name. His voice was hoarse, his accent strange.

My mother poured steaming coffee. "Drink this," she said, "talk later."

He warmed his hands on the fat mug. "My truck is stalled at the bottom of the hill, but I must get up to the McKenzie place," he said, speaking slowly. "Can't lose the day's work for a storm."

"Road's blocked," said my father. "You won't get through today."

"Oh I must!" he cried. "No work, no money. No money, no passage for my girl."

"You have a girl!" I said. "What's her name?"

George turned, and seemed to see me for the first time. "Her name is Karin. What is yours?"

"Stella," I told him, "and I can spell it backwards."

"I'm not surprised." He smiled a bit. "Karin spells, too. Even backwards."

"Well, where *is* Karin?" I demanded.

"Stella, hush!" warned my mother.

"Ah, but I like the questions children ask. They come from the heart," said George. "Karin is far away across the sea, where things are very bad for our people." He spoke quietly, taking care with his words. "She's in hiding now, with other Jewish children from our village."

"The war!" My parents were horrified.

"Is Karin afraid?" I whispered, licking my lips and knowing *I* would be.

"Karin is brave. She knows I will come for her. Just a little more time. A little more money...." George's voice trailed off.

"Let us help!" begged my parents. "We have some money saved."

But George pounded his muscle-fist on the table. "No charity!" he boomed, angry and proud. Frightened, too.

We were quiet for a while. What was there to say after all?

Then my mother had an idea. "George can build something here," she said, "in Stella's room perhaps. We can't pay much," she added, "but a day's work is a day's work."

So it was settled. George would build me a window seat. That very day.

He circled my room—I at his heels—tapping and rapping at walls and beams. "Every girl should have a place for dreaming," he told me as he lined his mouth with nails, "from birthday to birthday to birthday."

"Well, this one's ruined." I pouted. "No party *or* ring."

"What ring is that?" he asked.

I told him about the one in the window of Winston's. How I had saved and counted, for weeks and months. How I had planned to buy it this very morning. "Why couldn't it storm tomorrow," I sighed, "or the next day or next?"

"Sometimes," he answered, "you can't ask why."

And there was something in the way he said it that made me think rings and parties might not be so important after all.

"You must miss your girl," I said. "I wish I could help."

"You can." He handed me the hammer. "Hold it here like this, Stella, and bang these nails in place."

And I did. Again and again. Outside, that storm pelted the window. Bullets of ice air slipped through cracks I never knew were there. I was busy though, rubbing rolls of sandpaper until my fingers were roughened and stacks of wood were smooth as velvet.

"Is Karin pretty?" I wondered as we worked. "Tell me about her."

"Her eyes are bold and blue and they dance when she smiles. She's about your size, Stella, and before the bad times she went to school in a beautiful city with many river crossings. She likes hiking and chocolates and rings on her fingers."

"I like her already," I told him shyly. Across the room, I could see the bulging green pouch. Full of nickels. Just enough to buy the ring at Winston's.

At noon my
mother brought up
sandwiches. We ate lunch
picnic-style amongst the
scraps of wood. And after-
wards, the chocolate cake
with icing! George sanded. My
parents danced. I blew out the
candles. That year I made a
double wish. The usual
one for me. And one
for Karin, too.

All afternoon we sanded and sawed and measured and hammered. And just as a rainbow tinted the distant sky, my beautiful window seat was finished. I longed to try it with pillows, a blanket, and my favorite book. But first there was something I had to do.

While George packed up I secretly dropped my sack of nickels into his workbag, and I pinned a message to it.

Dear George,
    This is for Karin. I wish I could know her.
        Yours truly,
        Stella

For many weeks and even some months I listened at my window for George's truck. I suppose I thought he and Karin would appear—just like that—dancing up the path. But they never came.

I even saved more nickels.

Then one day, much later, my heart sank when I walked past Winston's and the ring was gone.

unt Stella stops the story but I want her to go on. "What happened to Karin! Did she come to this country? Was she safe? Did you meet her?"

"That's another story, Annie, for another time."

"But—"

"No buts." Aunt Stella pulls a tiny package from behind a pillow. Inside, tucked between plump chunks of cotton, is a ring of thinnest gold with a centered heart of darker gold and the initials SK in squiggly script. There is also an ancient note on yellow paper with fraying edges.

Dear Stella,

I am here in your country with my father. I am happy now. I hope you like this ring with your initial and mine.

Your friend,
Karin Rog

"The ring from Winston's!" I cry. "But how did Karin know?"

Aunt Stella rolls it onto my finger. "I've been saving it for you, Annie."

"I love it," I say, swallowing hard.

Aunt Stella smiles. "I knew you would." Then she picks up her fat book. "Go home for breakfast," she orders. "I've got reading to do."

I fluff the pillow behind her. "Don't forget about my party," I whisper. And I kiss her cheek.

"Haven't missed one yet."

I run down her hill, past the row of cherry trees, thinking of George and Karin. And of the little girl who was Aunt Stella, giving up all those nickels. I hold the ring to the lines of light, knowing I will never forget *this* story.

And when I am old I will tell it to someone smaller. The story of the ring and the window seat.